TO J.C.G.

Clarion Books
Ticknor & Fields, a Houghton Mifflin Company
Text copyright © 1984 by Beatrice Schenk de Regniers
Illustrations copyright © 1984 by Victoria de Larrea

Library of Congress Cataloging in Publication Data
de Regniers, Beatrice Schenk.
    Waiting for mama.

    Summary: Amy's wait outside the grocery store for
her mother seems interminable, and she spends the time
imagining the entire rest of her life.
    I. de Larrea, Victoria, ill.   II. Title.
PZ7.D4417Wai 1984   [E]   83-14982
ISBN 0-89919-222-X

Y   10 9 8 7 6 5 4 3 2 1

WAITING FOR MAMA

by Beatrice Schenk de Regniers

Illustrated by Victoria de Larrea

CLARION BOOKS

TICKNOR & FIELDS: A HOUGHTON MIFFLIN COMPANY

NEW YORK

"Wait here, Amy dear,"
says Amy's mother.
"I'll be right back.
Don't move!"

"Don't move?" Amy says.
"What if you don't come back?
Will I have to stay like this
for a hundred years?"

"Now Amy dear, don't be silly.
Don't I always come back
when I say I will come back?"

"Yes, Mama. You always come back."

"Well then, Amy, stay right on this bench
and wait for me. Officer Scott will be
here all the time. I'll be back in
ten minutes—maybe fifteen minutes."
And Amy's mother goes inside the grocery store.

Amy waits.

She waits...and waits...and waits.

"Mama always comes back," Amy tells her doll.

"We just have to wait."

Mrs. Gordon comes by.
"Amy! What are you doing here all alone?"

"I'm waiting," Amy says.
"Mama told me to wait for her."

Mr. Kassky comes by.
"Hi there, Amy," he says. "Having fun?"

"No," Amy says. "I'm waiting.
Mama told me to wait for her."

"That's fine," Mr. Kassky says.
"Have fun!"

John Clark comes by.

His mother is with him.

"Hi, Amy," he says.

"Look at my new running shoes.

I'll race you to the ice cream store!"

Amy looks at John Clark's new shoes.
"My mother is going to get me some shoes
just like yours," Amy says.

"Where is your mother, dear?"
Mrs. Clark asks.

"She's inside," Amy says.
"I'm waiting for her.
Mama told me to wait for her."

"Then you'd better stay right there,"
Mrs. Clark says.

"On your mark, get set, go!" John Clark says.
And he runs all the way to the ice cream store.

"Mama said ten minutes," Amy tells her doll.
"Or maybe fifteen minutes.
But I think we have been waiting
ONE HUNDRED minutes.
Maybe we will wait one hundred years."

"I will grow up and get married—"

"—and have lots of children.
But I will still be waiting.
My husband and children will wait, too."

"And every child will have a little dog.
And the dogs will have puppies.
And we will all be waiting—
        the puppies,
        the dogs,
        the children,
        and my husband,
        and I.
We will all be waiting and waiting."

"The children will grow up
and they will have children.
Then I will be a grandmother.
And I will still be waiting."

"And so will the children,
   and the grandchildren,
   and the dogs,
   and the puppies.
   My husband, too.
   We will all be waiting and waiting."

"We will wait for a hundred years."

"And one day, when I am a very old lady..."

Amy's mother comes out of
the supermarket.
"Oh, Amy dear! I'm afraid I was
away almost twenty minutes,"
she says.
"What a good girl you are!
Did you get tired waiting?
Were you lonely, dear?"

"I got tired waiting, Mama. But..."

"I wasn't lonely."